Endpapers by Eleanor Mensforth aged 10.
Thank you to St Bede's RC Primary School,
Jarrow, for helping with the endpapers
and the tastiest Coronation chicken – K.P.

For Margaret Coram, Winnie's greatest fan V.T.
To Oliver James Johnson K.P.

OXFORD
UNIVERSITY PRESS

Great Clarendon Street, Oxford OX2 6DP

Oxford University Press is a department of the University of Oxford.
It furthers the University's objective of excellence in research, scholarship,
and education by publishing worldwide in

Oxford New York
Auckland Cape Town Dar es Salaam Hong Kong Karachi
Kuala Lumpur Madrid Melbourne Mexico City Nairobi
New Delhi Shanghai Taipei Toronto

With offices in
Argentina Austria Brazil Chile Czech Republic France Greece
Guatemala Hungary Italy Japan Poland Portugal Singapore
South Korea Switzerland Thailand Turkey Ukraine Vietnam

Oxford is a registered trade mark of Oxford University Press
in the UK and in certain other countries

Text © Valerie Thomas 2005
Illustrations © Korky Paul 2005
The moral rights of the author and artist have been asserted
Database right Oxford University Press (maker)

First published in 2005
Reissued with new cover 2007

British Library Cataloguing in Publication Data available

ISBN 978–0-19-272726-8 (paperback)

ISBN 978–0-19-272725-1 (paperback with audio CD)

3 5 7 9 10 8 6 4

Printed in Singapore by Imago

www.korkypaul.com

Valerie Thomas and Korky Paul

Winnie at the Seaside

OXFORD

UNIVERSITY PRESS

It was a very hot summer.
Winnie the Witch felt hot and tired.
Wilbur, her cat, felt hot and tired, too.
'I want a swim, Wilbur,' Winnie said.
'Let's go to the seaside.'

Winnie found her beach towel, her
beach bag and her beach umbrella.

She jumped onto her broomstick,
Wilbur jumped onto her shoulder,
and they were off.

They flew over hot towns,
hot roads, hot cars,
and then they came to the sea.

There were lots of people on the beach,
but Winnie found a place for her towel.

She put up her beach umbrella
and got ready for her swim.

'Look after my bag and my broomstick, Wilbur,' Winnie said.
She ran into the water.

It was lovely in the sea.
Winnie splashed through the water,
and skipped over the little waves.
She was having a lovely time.

Wilbur sat and watched her.
He couldn't swim. He didn't like water.
He hated getting wet.

Winnie dived into the water. It was such fun!

But the water started to creep up the sand,
up to Winnie's towel.

Wilbur jumped onto
Winnie's beach umbrella.
'Meeow,' he cried.

Then the sea picked Winnie up, turned her
over three times, and dumped her on the sand.

The water washed over Winnie's towel,
and came half way up Winnie's beach bag.

'Meeeooooww,' cried Wilbur.
He didn't want to get wet.

'Oh dear,' said Winnie. She shook
some seaweed out of her hair.

'Don't worry, Wilbur.
   We'll just move further up the beach.'

She picked up her beach bag and her towel.
'My broomstick!' cried Winnie. 'Where's my broomstick?'

She looked everywhere.

No broomstick.

Then she looked out to sea.
There was her broomstick, floating away.

'Stop!' Winnie shouted.
But her broomstick didn't stop.

'How will we get home, Wilbur?' cried Winnie.
Then she had an idea.
She grabbed her beach bag, took out her
magic wand, waved it five times, and shouted,

ABRACADABRA!

The broomstick stopped.

Then it started to come back.

But a surfer was in the way.

WHOOSH

went the broomstick,
high up in the air,
and it landed on a whale.

The whale didn't want a broomstick on its back.

WHOOSH

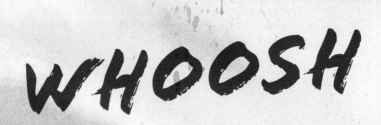

went the broomstick, high up in the air,
in a great spout of water.

SPLASH!

Winnie's broomstick had come back.
Winnie was pleased.

The other people on the beach
were not pleased at all.

They were very WET.

Wilbur was not pleased either.

He was very wet, very sandy,
and rather squashed.

'Oh dear,' Winnie said. 'We'd better go home, Wilbur.'
She packed everything up.

Then Winnie and Wilbur zoomed up into the sky.

They were soon home again.
It was still hot in Winnie's garden.
Winnie still felt hot and tired.

Then she had a wonderful idea.

She took her magic wand out of her beach bag,
shut her eyes, turned around three times,
and shouted,

ABRACADABRA!

There in her garden was
a beautiful swimming pool.

Winnie dived in.

She swam up and down, and
then she floated on her back.

'This is lovely, Wilbur,' she said.
'It's much nicer than the seaside.'

Anything is nicer than the seaside,
thought Wilbur.